A Taller tale of school

Graham White

Written & illustrated by Graham White
Edited by Dawn White

Charbel

happy reading

Graham

Copyright © 2017 G F White

All rights reserved. No part of this publication may be reproduced, distributed, or transmitted in any form or by any means, including photocopying, recording, or other electronic or mechanical methods, without the prior written permission of the publisher, except in the case of brief quotations embodied in critical reviews and certain other non-commercial uses permitted by copyright law. For permission requests, write to the publisher.

This book is dedicated to all who love to laugh, whatever their age.

Contents

Introduction 5
Clavertern School 7
The Head Master 10
The Cook 13
Lunch 16
School rules 20
A boy called Ray 22
The School inspection 25
The Kitchen accident 26
Let's look at the story a bit more 33
See if you can complete these sentences 37
What happened to the characters? 38
Joke 40

Introduction

I want to tell you a tale that will fill you with fear, about a school that is somewhere near here.

Built by the council on the edge of a Park
In a time when the council had a money to spend to keep it all
nice.
When the money ran out,
It turned grotty and grey

Unkempt and unloved it started to fester, with no budget to spend on keeping it right.

Clavertern School

In Clavertern town next to Clavertern park sat Clavertern school...... dreary, horrid, putrid, rotting and grey a visit to the school would surely darken your day.

It had sat on the edge of the park for longer than residents remember.

It had been there a decade or two, maybe three, or perhaps it was four?

No wait, it was definitely Five!

The school once had a playing field all neat and nice, it now had a field that was an explorers adventure.

Grass as high as your head, brambles that would cut you to shreds in the blink of an eye, A place that only the brave would dare try.

Rabbits, foxes and badgers now called home to a field that used to be mowed every week and kept very neat.

A trip to the field was not for the meek, the mild or the shy.
But rather a place where you train to survive!

The school could hardly be seen from the road, covered in mould, mosses, lichens and overgrown trees.

Brick work was slipping and cracking a lot, windows boarded and broken, trees growing in borders once planted with flowers and very neat shrubs.
Ivy was creeping all over the place gradually eating its way in.
All of this was before you got through the door!

We all know the rules, we all go to a school

Every boy every girl, an education to gain.

Poor kid or rich kid they all must go

If you were given a choice, you would give it a miss and decide not to go!

Clavertern school had teachers so cruel, every encounter left a dark and indelible mark on your soul!

A hideous Head Master and teachers as nasty as the look of the
Cook!

The Cook, ugly as Sin, she couldn't begin to serve up meals with any dietary appeal.

they were horrid, putrid and vile and what's more, they were very bad for your health.

Despite the complaining, the plotting, the scheming and getting in votes to have it demolished and finally closed,

Clavertern Town Council kept the school open……

it was cheaper to keep it and let it remain, than to demolish the School and start over again.

School starts in the morning and lasts all day long, with breaks

in between, with one they called……. lunch.

The Head Master

The Head Master was old and near to his end,

all crinkled, wrinkled and withered away.

His hair was flaky, horrid and grey and rather thin on the top.

His name was Mr Foster, he was twisted, wicked, nasty and cruel.

When it came to him speaking, he had nothing nice to say

there was no one alive who could ever remember a smile to have been seen on his face!

He employed staff with a frightening look.

They couldn't be nice nor even look good,

they had to look mean, be twisted, wicked,
Heartless and positively sadistic.

The boys and the girls had to quake in their shoes,

have good manners and always remember their
P's and their Q's.

The children looked forward to their breaks,

a chance to get out and away from the Grim
Reapers………. their Teachers

and their educational mistakes.

One break they feared though was their break
for lunch.

It meant they were expected to eat the food on
their plates,
all horrid, putrid, repugnant and vile.

The Cook

The cook at the school was a hideous, horrible sight, her hair was an oily mess, infested with very large lice.

her face looked like a road killed dead snake, everyone thought she had some kind of condition as her overall look wasn't great!

She had odd eyes that were bloodshot and sore,

one looked at you.................. the other the door!

She spoke with a slur and dribbled a lot,

the corner of her mouth was always awash,

it dribbled and ran down the side of her face, falling, you guessed it, all over the place.

her name fitted her horrid look,

she went by the name....... Ms McDrool.

Her hands were nasty, dirty, smelly and rot, oozing pus from the black heads that covered the skin on the back of her hands.

Her fingers were grubby, grimy and foul, it is doubtful if they'd ever been washed!

Oh sorry I forgot to say, as the budget was frightfully tight the Cook doubled as the cleaner of toilets at night!

It might explain the horrible look of her hands and I am sure you have guessed; she is dealing with toilets all covered in p...!

Lunch

Each child gets a heavy metal tray to carry their food,

two plates and a drink, is all it will take.

Each child staggering under its incredible weight.

The leftover Food gets recycled to keep down the waste.

The food on offer is a nutritional joy as I am sure you will agree when you see.

Here is a menu for you to savour and see.

Monday

Pig trotter broth, with maggot croutons.

Followed by.

Apple and earthworm turn over.

Tuesday

Baby wipe and lamb fat lasagne, with a veg peel salad.

Followed by.

Lemon stained finger nail and saw dust sponge.

Wednesday

Fish head and prawn tail soup.

Followed by.

Strawberry stalk ice cream.

Thursday

Lard burgers in cow pat buns.

Followed by.

Fermented orange peel sorbet.

Friday

Battered fish eye nuggets and frozen chips.

Followed by.

Custard lumps with apple peel and core pie.

To drink

Washed down by a drink of what they called milk.

It was closer to cheese, smelly, lumpy and not very nice.

As you can see the menu is a positive catering delight.

It would keep most sane adults awake every night.

In all of the years that McDrool ran the kitchen
Never once did a child ever ask her permission for more!

School rules

Now Foster and his team were a frightful bunch

They were sadistic, cruel, evil, nasty, bitter and twisted.

The rules you had to obey

Never be sick nor dare stay away.

Never miss a class or be last through the door.

Eat all of your lunch and never complain.

Speak when spoken to....... then never again.

Never run in a corridor unless you like pain.

While sitting in class you must clench your arse cheeks if you are in need of the Loo, as the answer for asking is always the same. No, never.......... never ask again!

When break time comes and you need the Loo, your worries have only just started to come to fruition.

By the way, it has nothing to do with a queue!

The toilets have all seen much better days, mould on the walls and generally damp from the leaky, overflowing drains, just entering the door makes you want to take a shower.

Only the desperate, risk a Clavertern school Loo, most hang on until home time and wait. Desperately clenching buttock cheeks at the school gate.

Despite a cleaner, the seats are a horrid and putrid affair, dirty and grimy, covered in mess. The bacteria count just has to be great

A boy called Ray

A boy called Ray, couldn't make the end of the day, desperate he entered the Loos at the afternoon break.

Picking the cleanest cubical he could find, with relief he squatted is bot on the seat,

with his job completed he risked his Bum on the school Loo paper.

Very few do.

With a pull on the chain, he thought he was done,

but no, he was then caught out by the rotten wall as the cistern decided to fall, dislodged by the pull on the chain.

Knocked clean out by the bang on the head, Ray lay there unconscious....... not dead; in the dirt and the grime on the floor, until McDrool arrived to clean the toilets at 9.

McDrool arrived at 9 on the dot, bucket and mop she started to flop water around on the floor.

A quick push on each cubical door, a flip and a flop of the mop.

Door four was a challenge as Ray was a wedge, larger than most boys his age.

McDrool gave it a shove and found Ray out cold on the floor.

Now McDrool might be slow when it comes to the food, but given this situation she sprang straight into emergency action, tipping the dirty mop bucket over Rays head!

Ray came too as the water soaked through coughing, choking and rubbing his eyes.

Poor Ray now had a lump, from the bump on his head and an odour that announced, he might even be dead!

Back on his feet he decided to leave, he went home very late in a very sorry state and a terrible mess with a huge swollen lump on his head.

The School inspection

Surprisingly the school passed every inspection,
a feat that was put down to luck on reflection.

When the school inspectors came calling they
used a SATNAV to find their way.
but by default it sent them the wrong way.

You would have thought they would have
known it was wrong and corrected the mistake,
but no, the inspectors were terribly lazy.

So they filled out the forms to give them a
Grade,
then went to the next job instead!

The Kitchen accident

Mc Drool had an accident in the kitchen one day, she was bent over, looking into the oven when some of her head lice jumped ship!

The lice crawled through grease in the oven then up the gas pipe blocking it tight.

Try as she might the oven wouldn't light, so not to be defeated she increased the pressure in the pipe!
Now the pipe was fully loaded, she struck up a match.
there was a huge explosion, it really was an incredible sight!

A mushroom cloud rose high in the sky over the town.

The walls of the kitchen, all blown away to leave a frightful sight, McDrool flat on the floor, head in the oven with all her clothes alight.

Foster heard the screaming from his office down the hall,
As fast as his legs would carry him he was first at the door.
He grabbed a pot of stew and doused McDrool down.
She was now flame free but covered in a stinky cold stew, a very
special kind of goo!
The fire brigade arrived with big blue flashing lights.

An ambulance was called to collect McDrool, she was still a very unpleasant sight.

When they arrived she was still laying stuck in the goo.
The smell was a mix of cooking gas and putrid rotting food, so bad that the emergency services didn't know exactly what to do.

Eventually the Army came to see what they could do.

McDrool was deemed a hazard, the fire brigade hosed her down, the ambulance then took her to the hospital in a special rubber isolation gown, to a very special unit, where they deal with serious chemical hazards.

The school was declared a dangerous site, all the staff and children were evacuated out into the night.

The Army Major arrived to have a better look, he arrived in a Land rover packed with loads of dynamite.

Troops were everywhere, digging lots of little holes.

Each hole was given a stick of dynamite,
When all the sticks were buried the major was informed.

The major pressed a button, a very loud bell was sounded twice, a warning to all around that he was about to press the……. detonation button!

Two minutes later the plunger was depressed.

There was a huge explosion, the second of the day.
Another large mushroom cloud high in the sky, above the town.

Bricks and mortar were spread across the site, where the school once stood there was now a massive hole,

(I am sure you could have seen it from deep in outer space).
Clavertern school demolished, it had finally gone away. Ray and the other children had survived to tell the tale and live another day!

The End

Let's look at the story a bit more

1. What was the name of the school?

2. Can you remember the name of the Park?

3. What was the name of the name of the Head Teacher?

4. Can you remember the name of the Cook?

5. What was on the menu for Monday?

6. What drink did the boys and girls get with their lunch?

7. What hit Ray on the head?

8. What time did the cleaner start cleaning?

9. What blocked the cooker gas pipe?

10. What did the fire brigade do to the cook?

11. What did the Army major arrive in?

12. What finally happened to the school?

See if you can complete these sentences

If you were given a choice, you would give it a miss and _____ _____.

It was cheaper to keep it and let it remain, than to _____ _____.

Have good manners and always remember their P's and their ___.

The cook at the school was a hideous, horrible sight, her hair was an oily mess, _____.

What happened to the characters?

You may be wondering as to the fate of the characters in our story.

McDrool is still in an isolation unit because of her vile smell.

They tried to get her clean, even though it was rather mean, they pressure washed her with an industrial pressure washing machine.

Mr Foster is in his own sort of Goo, he has been sent to prison,
With no chance of remission.

Ray recovered well, but still smells rather strange, a constant memory of the fateful night, when McDrool washed him down; positively turning him a dirtier shade of brown.

Joke

Three friends set sail to travel the world, one night there was a terrible storm. They had to abandon ship.

They were washed up on a tropical island. The island was quite small but had fresh water and they found food to eat.

One day while walking along the shore they found a small oil lamp.

They rubbed it clean and POOF a genie appeared.

"I can grant each of you only one wish."

The first man wished he was back home safe. POOF and he was home.

The second man wished he too could be home with his friend. POOF and he was home.

The third man thought for a while, then said, "I feel lonely here on my own, I wish my friends were still with me." POOF
The three friends were all together again on the island.

Be careful what you wish for!

Printed in Great Britain
by Amazon